The GREEDY SPARROW

AN ARMENIAN TALE

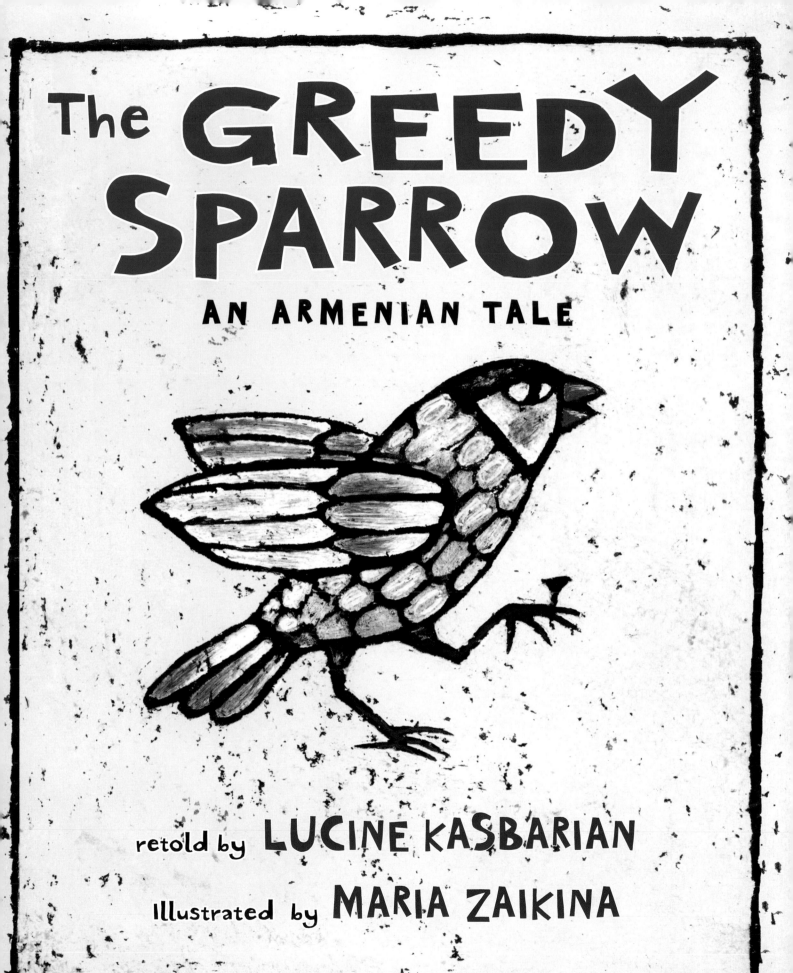

retold by LUCINE KASBARIAN

Illustrated by MARIA ZAIKINA

Marshall Cavendish Children

Author's Note

Armenian fables begin with "Once there was and was not"
to suggest that fantastical tales may be real or imagined. The
fable of the sparrow, which has been in the Armenian oral
tradition for centuries, was first put to paper by the Armenian
poet, Hovhannes Toumanian (1869–1923). In *The Greedy
Sparrow*, an original composition, we learn that people who
engage in dishonest or selfish behavior may end up losing
whatever they gained because of that behavior.

Text copyright © 2011 by Lucine Kasbarian
Illustrations copyright © 2011 by Maria Zaikina
Marshall Cavendish Corporation, 99 White Plains Road, Tarrytown, NY 10591
www.marshallcavendish.us/kids

Library of Congress Cataloging-in-Publication Data

Kasbarian, Lucine.
The greedy sparrow : an Armenian tale / by Lucine Kasbarian ; illustrated
by Maria Zaikina. – 1st ed.
p. cm.
Summary: A sparrow receives kindness from strangers and repays each act of
kindness with a trick to get more, but at last, in a surprising twist, the
sparrow is back with his original problem.
ISBN 978-0-7614-5821-0
[1. Greed–Fiction. 2. Sparrows–Fiction.] I. Zaikina, Maria, ill. II.
Title.
PZ7.K1532Gr 2011
[E]–dc22
2010018172

The art was rendered with layers of wax and oil paint, and then the layers were cut away to reveal the colors underneath.
Book design by Anahid Hamparian
Editor: Margery Cuyler

Printed in China (E)
First edition
1 3 5 6 4 2

mc **Marshall Cavendish**
Children

To my Armenian forebears, great-grandmother, and father, all of whom preserved the sparrow fable through the ages.

"Guide the seed carefully and the tree will grow upright."

–Armenian Proverb

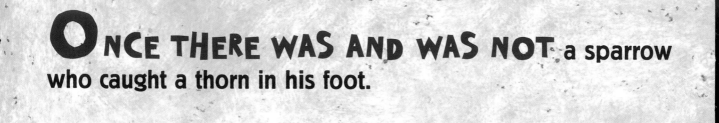

ONCE THERE WAS AND WAS NOT a sparrow who caught a thorn in his foot.

He flew and flew until he spotted a woman baking bread.

The baker removed the thorn,
and the sparrow flew away.

The baker tossed the thorn into the oven and got back to work.

The baker saw that it was no use arguing, so she gave the sparrow some bread.

The sparrow dropped the bread into the shepherd's hands and flew away.

And that's just what he did.

The shepherd saw that it was no use arguing, so he handed over a sheep to the sparrow.

The sparrow picked up the sheep and carried it off.

They flew over Mount Ararat and Lake Van until they came to a wedding celebration on the Armenian island of Aghtamar.

They landed next to the bride and groom.

As the sparrow flew away, the guests sang, danced, and made merry until all the food was gone.

While the groom danced, he eyed the sheep.

WHAT WOULD HAPPEN IF I SLAUGHTERED THE SHEEP, GRILLED IT, AND MADE SHISH KEBAB FOR ALL THE GUESTS?

And that's just what he did.

WE RAN OUT OF FOOD AT THE WEDDING, SO WE SLAUGHTERED THE SHEEP, GRILLED IT, AND MADE SHISH KEBAB FOR ALL THE GUESTS.
EITHER YOU GIVE ME MY SHEEP OR YOU GIVE ME THE BRIDE!

Seeing that there was no use arguing, the groom surrendered his bride.

The sparrow and the bride traveled the mountains and valleys of the Caucasus.

The sparrow left the bride with the minstrel and flew away.

As the minstrel sang to himself, he became so enchanted with his melody that he forgot about the bride.

Seeing this, the bride stole away to return to her groom.

Seeing that there was no use arguing, the minstrel gave the sparrow his lute.

The sparrow took the lute by its strings and flew over the mountains.

In the distance, he saw an apricot tree overlooking the shores of Lake Sevan.

He rested on a thorny branch, strummed his lute, smiled to himself, and began to chirp. . . .

IN PLACE OF A THORN, I GOT SOME BREAD. IN PLACE OF SOME BREAD, I GOT A SHEEP. IN PLACE OF A SHEEP, I GOT A BRIDE. IN PLACE OF A BRIDE, I GOT A LUTE. AND NOW . . . I AM . . . A MINSTREL!

But as the sparrow rocked in glee, he lost his footing, and the lute fell, too, leaving the sparrow as he began . . . with nothing but a thorn in his foot!